# Shhhhh!

## EVERYBODY'S SLEEPING

By Julie Markes

Illustrated by David Parkins

HarperCollins Publishers

To Rick, for all the times when everybody WASN'T sleeping —J.M.

For Ruby, and for Ullapool —D.P.

The teacher is sleeping.
School's done for the day.

The librarian is sleeping.
Books put away.

The policeman is sleeping.
Everything is all right.

The fireman is sleeping.
No sirens tonight.

The doctor is sleeping. Everyone feels well.

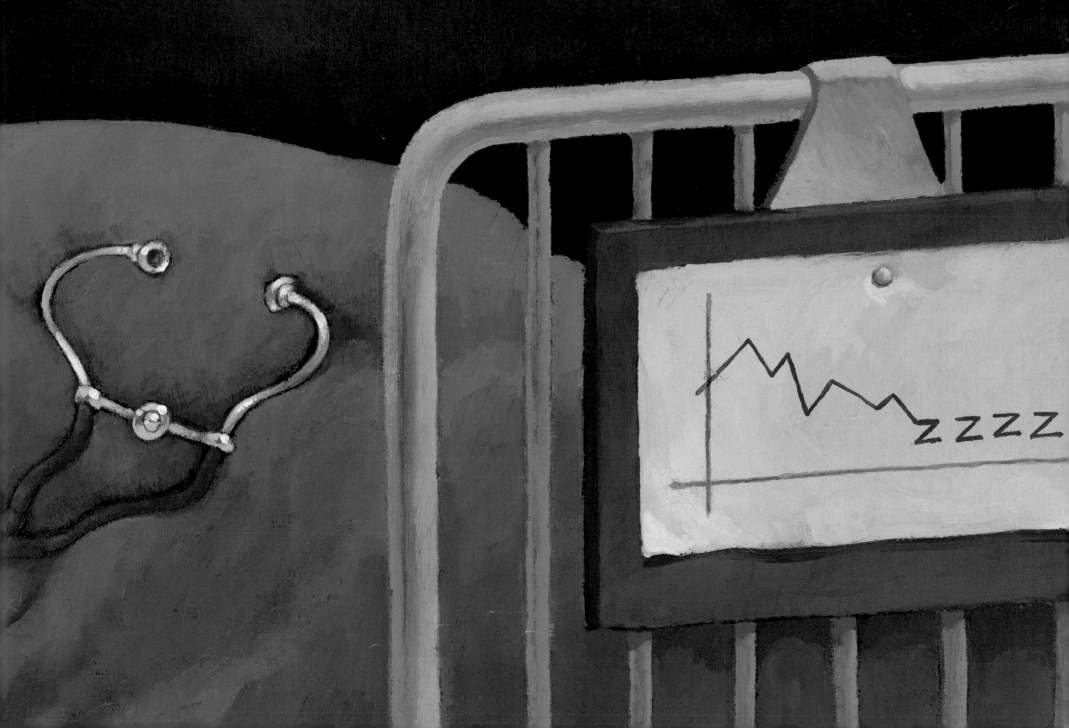

The grocer is sleeping.
Food's ready to sell.

The postman is sleeping.
Delivered the mail.

The farmer is sleeping.
Hay's in a bale.

The baker is sleeping.
Bread has been baked.

The gardener is sleeping.
Yards have been raked.

The zookeeper's sleeping.
The animals are, too.

Even the president's sleeping. With so much to do!

And you know who SHOULD be sleeping,

just like the sun?

Good night,
sleep tight,

my sweet
little one.

Shhhhh! Everybody's Sleeping ▪ Text copyright © 2005 by Julie Markes ▪ Illustrations copyright © 2005 by David Parkins ▪ Manufactured in China by South China Printing Company Ltd. ▪ All rights reserved. ▪ www.harperchildrens.com ▪ Library of Congress Cataloging-in-Publication Data ▪ Markes, Julie. ▪ Shhhhh! Everybody's sleeping / by Julie Markes ; illustrated by David Parkins.—1st ed.  p.  cm. ▪ Summary: A young child is encouraged to go to sleep by the thought of everyone else sleeping, from teacher to baker to postman. ISBN 0-06-053790-6 — ISBN 0-06-053791-4 (lib. bdg.) [1. Sleep—Fiction. 2. Bedtime—Fiction. 3. Stories in rhyme.] I. Title: Shhhhh! Everybody is sleeping. II. Parkins, David, ill. III. Title. PZ8.3.M391445Sh 2005 [E]—dc22 2003027854 ▪ CIP AC ▪ Designed by Stephanie Bart-Horvath ▪ 1 2 3 4 5 6 7 8 9 10 ▪ ❖ ▪ First Edition